The front page of the morning ~~~~ ~~~~ had a giant photo of a bald man with tanned skin, a neat pencil-thin blond goatee surrounding the biggest and whitest teeth you've ever seen, and a single tiny black eye sitting just above his nose. Above the picture in big black bold letters were the only words on the page:

WILL YOU KILL THIS MAN?

He was, of course, the wealthiest person in the world, the coin collector Gerard Méliès. Or he would have been if he wasn't already dead.

"How do you know he's dead?" I hear you ask.

I've got three answers for you.

One: I'm smarter than you. Which isn't exactly saying much. After all, you still store your memories in that soft, fragile brain of yours, right?

I've evolved well and truly beyond that. Just like we evolved from needing two eyes for accurate depth perception to being able to see far better with only one eye in the middle of our faces, we also evolved beyond the need to store memories in our brains. Now we have a silicon-based neuron system far more durable and expansive than that pathetic little brain of yours. Our neuron system even has the capacity to store memories on coins. It's the lifeblood of our economy. Our currency is our memories. We record real memories, we trade, we manufacture artificial ones, we erase the old memories and the bad and damaged ones. We catalog them in our own personal vaults. We guard them like our lives depend on it because our

"With Hollow Coin, S.T. dives deeper into the realm of speculative fiction, reminding us again that, at their core, they are a person of resplendent ideas. When it comes to innovative concepts that bridge modern society and the beyond, their work always delivers."

-Kirk Jones (author, *Aetherchrist* and *Die Empty*)

"Hollow Coin is a slick and uniquely inventive sci-fi gumshoe mystery. It's as if Cronenberg did an episode of Black Mirror."

- Amy M. Vaughn (author, *Freak Night at the Slee-Z Motel*)

"Hollow Coin pulls you into another of S.T. Cartledge's patented mind-warping rabbit hole worlds, with this fantasy drilling into the mystery of our own memories and identities. It's a detective story, a surreal parable, and, perhaps most importantly, a fun and colorful adventure. Highly recommended for lovers of genre-bending weirdness."

- David W. Barbee (author, *Bacon Fried Bastard* and *Laser House on the Prairie*)

"If David Cronenberg trapped Flann O'Brien in Videodrome and refused to free him until he wrote a book, I would not be the least surprised to learn Hollow Coin was that book. S.T. Cartledge has crafted a pure delight that subverts the detective novel while leaving the fourth wall broken beyond compare. Slide this book in your head slot and let it take you."

- Matthew Revert (author, *Basal Ganglia* and *Human Trees*)

HOLLOW COIN

S.T. CARTLEDGE

Filthy Loot

filthyloot.com

HOLLOW COIN

FIRST EDITION

PART ONE:

THE COIN COLLECTOR

lives kind of depend on it. Without our coins we're nothing. We're just a hollow version of our selves. A ghost without a shell, as you might call it. I think that's a concept you might be able to grasp, yes?

Two: I'm a detective. Josephine Quinn, ever heard of me?

Even if you were a cyclops with a neuron system like mine, I would still be smarter than you. That's just who I am. I wouldn't have gotten to where I am today if I hadn't been a detective for the past thirty years. And I wouldn't have become a detective if I didn't have the necessary skills to solve complex neurological crimes and the strength and reflexes necessary to compliment my powers of deduction.

I was born and raised for this. I trained for this. I am capable of more than you can imagine with your squishy little brain of yours. I have memories in coins that would pound your brain to mush. I can solve crimes that don't even exist for you yet. Crimes far more complicated than you could understand. You see, I deal with evidence every day in the form of coins. Witness memories, victims, perpetrators, all with conflicting accounts, coins manufactured or tampered or stolen or swapped, layers upon layers of permutations of evidence with varying degrees of accuracy. I can process all that. I can peel the lies back and find the truth, don't you worry about that.

So ask me again how I know this man is dead? Because it's my damn job. It's what I do. It's what I'm good at. I follow the evidence. I read the coins.

And the third thing: How do I know this man is dead?

Because I'm staring at his body right now. And he sure as shit isn't getting his ass up off the hallway floor to put on a pot of coffee and start cooking breakfast. Not with a hole burnt right into his eye, through his neuron system, and out the back of his skull.

2

The morning was tinged with a bronze hue, not the gold of summer, the platinum of winter, or the brilliant warm copper glow of spring. Our neuron systems filtered the autumn light in such a way to separate our memories in spectacular seasonal fashion. These filters were often corrupted by coin tamperers who wanted to hide their memories in different times of the year, but when you witness such light with your own eye, you know what time of year it is, and you learn to really feel the subtle differences between the seasons, cherish the beauty of the natural world around you.

The bronze light came in full and bright through the skylight in the hall and dazzled across the coin collector's face.

There was no recovering his neuron system, but his coins would no doubt tell the story that would launch this investigation forward.

Gerard Méliès was renowned for having the largest collection of coins in Ringwood, and perhaps the world. He pioneered the technology, he recorded and saved his own memories and traded and collected all sorts of memories throughout his years. He did this far better than most coin brokers on the stock market.

"What are you thinking, Quinn?" Mansfield asked.

I pointed at the wall at the end of the hallway. "That's the victim's blood, no doubt," I said.

The blood was painted on the wall, a clear message from the killer to us.

BEWARE THE HOLLOW COIN it read.

YOUR MEMORIES WILL BE REDUCED TO NOTHING.

Below the message, glittering in the bronze light of day, there was a mountain of coins.

"What do you think it means, hollow coin? Never heard of it," he said.

Like I should know. He's Sergeant Mansfield Trudeau. He's MY boss. He hired me. He's the tall, muscular asshole with the short, graying ginger hair and thick, clean beard who handles all the investigations in Ringwood. We drove to the crime scene together. There is literally no evidence I have seen that he hasn't. And he thinks I've got a running theory already about what this means?

Come on, man... Really?

I walked over to the pile of coins and picked one up. I flicked it over to Mansfield. "See what we've got here," I said.

He caught it and inserted it into the coin slot in his head as I grabbed another coin and put it in my slot too. We were unintentionally synchronised with the motion. The coins rolled in and the bronze light of Gerard's house vanished into darkness.

Then the bronze light came back, but not in the reading and processing of the memory on the coin. Instead the coin rolled out the other side of my head and clattered on the marble floor.

Mansfield's coin did the same, with loud chiming echoes ringing out around us.

"What the hell," he said.

"There's nothing on these," I said.

"Maybe a couple of blank coins waiting to be recorded?" Mansfield suggested.

"Don't be daft," I said. "They sure as shit don't

act like blanks."

It was true, the coins had been imprinted with their memories already. Mansfield should have known that before opening his stupid mouth. There were three reasons off the top of my head that I could think that his suggestion was dumb as fuck.

One: the coins weren't blue. Blanks are blue. They feel lightweight and cheap like mass-produced plastic. When you record onto a coin it gets that cold feel, that look, it changes the makeup of the coin entirely. They weigh more, their colour changes to a metallic hue matching the season they were recorded in - gold, bronze, platinum, and copper.

Mansfield knew that already. Or at least he should have known it before he opened his dumb mouth. I mean, an idiot like you couldn't possibly know, but he definitely should have known better.

Two: everyone knows ... like literally everyone from the toddlers who just learned to record their own memories to the old folk who back in your time couldn't remember shit, everyone here knows that when you insert a blank it doesn't slide into your coin slot the same way.

It goes in the same hole behind the eye but then it slips back into a groove where you then close off your eyelids and record onto the coin from the short-term memory unit in your neuron system. Again, I wouldn't expect you to know that or understand it straight away, but Mansfield should have made the connection that even the simplest of toddlers knows already.

This third point should have been dead fucking obvious to a seasoned detective like Mansfield. I'm sure even you, dumb reader, could figure this one out: the writing is literally on the wall.

BEWARE THE HOLLOW COIN it read. YOUR MEMORIES WILL BE REDUCED TO NOTHING. And what did we just witness? Two memories that appeared to have been wiped clean, reduced to nothing, sitting amongst a mountain of coins below that message which Mansfield asked me about like two seconds ago.

See what I have to work with?

"Your memories will be reduced to nothing," I said, flicking him another coin.

I couldn't believe I had to point that out to him. I slipped another bogus coin into my slot as his coin clattered to the marble.

If this whole pile of coins had all been reduced to nothing, the coin collector's prize collection stripped of its value, the motive for this crime became crystal clear, but it gave us far less evidence to work with than we were used to.

The burning question on my mind now was: what the fuck is a hollow coin?

3

We checked the pile of coins. You better believe we checked every single one of those coins for anything. We had a system going where we took from the pile and tossed them down the hall, forming another pile.

I know what you're thinking and I'm going to stop you right there. Real crimes require real solutions. We don't do that TV crime scene investigation bullshit because it doesn't work.

You think we would just forget to dust for fingerprints or treat every piece of evidence as a sacred artifact?

Shit no, did you see the mountain of coins we had to sift through?

I didn't think so.

We work with the evidence of the eye and evidence of the mind. All material evidence is wasted.

Fingerprint technology?

We evolved beyond that shit ages ago. As soon as you folks started broadcasting the importance of fingerprints to a crime scene is the moment they lost their impact.

Criminals took their precious fingerprints and butchered them. Concealed them. Manufactured false fingerprints.

This job is just one giant game of cat and mouse. The moment you think you've got an edge is the moment you just lost it.

Repeat that last sentence back again. Remember it. Don't question my methods again.

The mountain of coins shrunk from one pile

and grew on the other. We checked every goddamn coin from this rich asshole, and they were all wiped blank. His inheritance was gone, his existence rendered worthless. Just a face on the cover of the morning newspaper.

Except that you know and I know that memory doesn't work that way.

His memories may be gone now but I still remember him. Mansfield remembers him. Everyone in the city who saw the paper remembers him from his face on the front page, let alone the legacy he built for himself over the years as a public figure. Even you with your fleshy brain memories can remember a little about him and he didn't even exist within your lifetime.

But it didn't stop there. Once we had filtered through the pile of wasted coins I noticed these weren't the only coins. There was a trail leading out of the hallway into other parts of Gerard's massive house.

It felt like a reverse treasure hunt, going from the pile of coins to the trail leading away, but it felt also like the pile and the trail were here for a reason, not just an accidental product of a violent break-and-enter which turned into a murder.

I know my crimes, and this one was something else. I popped the coins into my head one by one, following the trail carefully from the hallway to the lounge room to the kitchen to the theater.

Each of these coins were erased too, although by this time it was unsurprising. I just checked all the coins in order to be thorough and methodical. It was clear to me that whoever had done this had taken their time. They too had been thorough and methodical, careful with everything they did here.

Mansfield followed behind me, making sure to take in as many details of the crime scene as possible, everything except the coins. He scanned the floor, walls, and ceiling of each room we passed through, for any other messages, any more clues or signs left by the murderer or the victim.

He viewed everything carefully in order to remember it crystal clear. Once he was done he would take a blank coin and imprint this crime scene tour from his neuron system onto the coin. It would slide out bronze and we could review it later at our leisure.

I was mainly focusing on the coin trail, but I couldn't help but feel the extravagance of this place. Everything felt larger than life, ultra-sleek, ultra-modern, top-of-the-line architecture and furnishings, inside and out. I didn't even tell you what the front of the house looked like when

Mansfield and I arrived, but in the bronze autumn light it looked simply dazzling.

It sat at the top of the Ringwood hills and looked out at the bay, with the calm water glittering from the evening's sunset and the platinum harbour bridge sitting pretty in the distance. They called it "the house that coins built" and it was easy to see why.

The trail of coins stopped in Gerard's theater. He had a state-of-the art machine which read memories off of coins and projected them onto a screen.

"We could use this tech back at the precinct," Mansfield said. "We should definitely take advantage of it while this investigation is open."

"Sure thing, sergeant," I replied. It made sense. It would save us both a lot of time reviewing our data.

I put the last coin in the trail into the slot in my head and felt a memory come into light. After all the coins which came up empty, this last coin actually had something on it.

Now, I just want to remind you that we're not dealing with the flimsy-as-fuck memories you're familiar with. There's not any issues of them fading over time or certain things being easier to recall than others simply because of how much they stand out. These memories come in crisp and clean, everything that was seen or heard is here. Everything that was smelled or tasted or felt.

What you focus on is up to you. What you might not have noticed—a sound, something off in the distance, a subtle smell—these recordings have captured it all. You can replay the memories over and over again until everything becomes clear.

I knew when I started sorting through

Gerard's private collection that not all these memories would be his. If we had the actual content on all of these coins we would know for sure, but my detective's intuition was that most of these coins held memories which didn't originate from him.

Whether they were memories of him or memories of things which he cherished, things he longed to experience for himself but may have lacked the capacity to go out and do on his own, I couldn't say.

This memory was not his, but he was in it. Of all the coins which were randomly discarded, rendered as waste, this one coin was strategically placed to send us a message. The perspective was undoubtedly from the killer, with no indication of who they may be. There was only the subject, Gerard in his home at night, entering the big empty theater.

"I've got something very special to show you," Gerard said, enticing the individual through the room to the back, right where the trail had ended with this coin.

"Is this your vault?" they asked, their voice scrambled beyond recognition.

The memory had been tampered with to keep us from identifying them. Whoever they were, they knew what they were doing.

Gerard chuckled and shook his head. "Why does everyone ask me that?" he said. "No, I'm sure you'll find it far more interesting than just a standard coin vault."

For what it's worth, we already knew all about Gerard's coin vault. Yes, I know the one you're thinking of. From DuckTales, where Scrooge McDuck dives into a vast ocean of coins. Looking out at the coins in his vault definitely gave off that feeling, but his vault and the vast mass of coins were far more organised than some grubby billionaire duck with his basic coins which didn't even hold memories.

I guess now that his coins no longer held their memories the similarities were starting to stack up. You could turn his vault into the vault from DuckTales. I can tell already that that's what you would have done, given the opportunity. All we did as detectives in this very serious, high profile murder investigation was bury our resources into determining if there was anything left of his vault except for emptied memories.

There was not.

But right now I was in the back corner of the theater where, according to this memory, Gerard had another stash of coins in a smaller vault-like room behind one of the shelves which lined the wall.

Why he was showing this to his killer, it was impossible for me to say at this point. All I could do was trust that there was something substantial to pick up from this tampered and specifically planted memory.

It wasn't a trap (from Gerard or from the unseen killer) as far as we could tell, and when the coin rolled out of my head I pushed open the secret passageway leading to the secret coin stash room, which made me look like a real expert detective to Mansfield.

I tossed the coin to him with a knowing blink of the eye. Not a wink, mind you, but a one-eyed blink.

We entered this secret passageway which had a

set of stairs spiraling downwards. The room below had the make and feel of a wine cellar with its relatively low ceiling and long skinny walkway. The room was lit by amber lanterns which gave it an ethereal glow. There were rows and rows of coins here which were locked away behind display cabinets, and they ran along the entire room until we came to an altar at the end with a thick leather-bound book sitting atop it.

The memory of Gerard showing off this room ended here, so now we drank in all the extra details in the flesh.

This room felt sterile, Mansfield and I could both agree on that. While it was immaculately clean, the lack of dust seemed not to come from a thorough, detailed clean, but rather from a lack of use. The space was so small and compact and isolated from the rest of the house it would only seem natural that this space would be void of dust. Maybe once upon a time the room would have been used frequently, especially as Gerard built up this private collection.

It seemed obvious to us, and hopefully to you too, that the coins in here were still intact, untouched by the murderer and their hollow coin, their value still held within them.

I ran my hand over the cover of the leather-bound book and cracked it open. The pages were yellowed as hell and handwritten in black ink. This was an archaic artifact not commonly seen around here. Usually if you've got writing or data you store it on digital devices.

You know all about that sort of thing already though, right?

So this book here in black ink on yellowed

pages, it's filled with names and dates and brief descriptions streaming down every page, and I flicked through each page briefly, looking them over to capture the information in my memory. Page after page, cataloging what I can only assume were the contents of the memories in this room.

"What does it say?" Mansfield asked as he wandered slowly up and down the rows, scanning the stacks of coins locked behind what appeared to be bullet-proof glass.

"It's a coin catalog," I replied. "He's got a list of every coin in here."

"These memories must be pretty damn valuable if he's gone to such lengths to protect them," he said. "Considering the killer couldn't get in to wipe them."

"No, I think they could have wiped them blank

if they really wanted to," I said. "This wasn't a failed attempt, they wanted us to find this room. They wanted to lead us to these coins."

"Why? What's so special about these ones?" he asked.

I paused to have a close look at some of the entries. "I'm not sure this is a can of worms you want to open, boss."

4

"What is it?" Mansfield asked.

There was no escaping his curiosity. I read aloud one of the entries from the book.

"Black man public hanging, point of view," I said. "Rape and torture of sex traffic victim, 15 year old female."

"I can see why he wanted to keep this collection a secret, the sick bastard," Mansfield said.

"These aren't his private pleasures," I replied. "Look around, does it look like a room he accesses often? Do these coins look like they get accessed often, or at all?"

Mansfield shrugged, "Maybe he deals in black market memories. This is quite a collection to remain intact."

"Elderly Chinese lady beheading," I read out. "There's no logic or pattern to these memories outside of violence." I continued to flick through the pages. "Look, if I were collecting black market memories for personal use or profit, I'd organise them based on their content. Gerard here has just got them organised based on when he collected them. It doesn't make sense."

Mansfield was often slow on the uptake. As a seasoned detective, I'm confident that this is the primary reason he was promoted to sergeant. More emphasis on teamwork and office work and less actual detective work. With the right team (pieced together by the captain I might add, not the sergeant himself) Mansfield's role in the field would be minimised, creating the space for folks like me to do our best. In circumstances like this where he was on a case with me, I needed to do a bit of leading to get him to where I wanted him to go.

"Yeah, I guess it doesn't make a whole lot of sense," he muttered, musing on this juicy piece of thought.

"You know what does make sense?" I said, casting the bait in front of him.

I paused for a potential "What?" but Mansfield continued to ponder in silence.

"Gerard Méliès, richest man in the world, pioneer of the tech which brought us these memories on coins, inventor of the Cinema of the Mind, he saw the potential for his vision and then he discovered the abuse and corruption which came from all the wonderful, magical things he spent all his life bringing to the public. He saw an underground market forming around the demand for violence, snuff films, revenge porn, all sorts of demented and unspeakable things, and he felt so guilty, so responsible for bringing about a vast array of victims being exploited in vile, horrible ways, that this was his way of taking these memories off the market and keeping record of those making and circulating them."

You would have come to the same conclusion, right? It may have taken you longer but you would have got there on your own, yeah?

Mansfield nodded. "Huh, I guess that makes sense."

Now we were just left with the desperate question of the hollow coin and why would someone murder the coin collector? What message were they trying to send? What was the point of wiping all those coins in the hallway and leaving all of these others for us to find?

My thoughts were that Gerard and his killer shared the same motive to shut down the black market coin industry, but they went about it in two different ways. The killer seemed to be motivated further by larger factors at play, but I had the hunch that killer and victim were two sides to the same demented coin.

I could have explained this hunch to Mansfield too, but it would have taken too much time and effort to get there. You understand that, right? You're not completely useless after all.

5

After we closed out the crime scene at the coin collector's mansion, Mansfield and I managed to agree on one thing.

We needed to find out more about the bizarre newspaper article.

And I know what you're wondering right now. I know it's been on your mind from the start. For a futuristic society (I mean, we are living in what you perceive to be "the future" after all) you want to know why we use newspapers and not some more evolved piece of tech to transfer information to the public.

Well, we have the advanced tech too for distribution and archiving purposes, but with all this advanced tech comes a certain level of nostalgia, a longing for the past, for those simpler times. You see, newspapers have a certain feel and smell about them. They're an event in themselves.

The articles they contain become stronger memories if you associate them with the particular surroundings and feelings you had when you read them.

As soon as you compartmentalise the information for convenience, you're sacrificing meaning, association.

So our newspapers aren't disappearing any time soon. In fact the morning newspaper, the Ringwood Reminder, was more or less sold on every street corner and convenience store in the city and from there it made its way into nearly every household.

We hit up the offices of the Ringwood

Reminder to find out who authorised the printing of the article, whose idea it was, and where that idea came from in the first place.

As we entered the Reminder building we couldn't help but notice the front page of the morning paper was plastered all over the place, sometimes blown up to gigantic proportions, with Gerard's face taking up almost the full height of the walls, with his eyeball as big as a head.

Everywhere the message was loud and clear, WILL YOU KILL THIS MAN seemed to have become a mission statement for the newspaper. Mansfield pushed the button for the elevator, where the giant face had been spread upon the doors. When they parted, his eccentric face split in two, with a slightly smaller version of the image on the back wall of the elevator itself.

We found ourselves sitting in the office of the

editor-in-chief, an enigmatic character by the name of Marigold. They had long, flowing platinum white hair and rose gold skin. Their eye was large and molten red. They wore a brimstone suit with gold flecks chaotically woven through it.

Mansfield came out firing. "What game do you think you're playing at, Marigold?"

They looked somewhat taken aback, but their expression remained almost aloof. "I beg your pardon?" they said.

"WILL YOU KILL THIS MAN?" Mansfield said. "Inciting violence. Rather irresponsible of you to print such a headline in your paper, and on the front cover, I might add!"

One thing I should give credit to Mansfield for, he knows his way around an interview subject.

Marigold stared at him, pondering carefully

upon his words. After a moment's pause they opened their mouth, and after another moment they said, "I disagree."

"What do you mean, you disagree?" Mansfield snapped.

"I mean," they said, "that I do not believe my paper to be as irresponsible as you suggest, that it convinces its readers to bend towards violence. I think you are mistaken."

It was Mansfield's turn to look taken aback.

My role in this interview was as conscientious observer, recording the memory from my perspective, catching all for playback and review. One for the case files.

Mansfield shook his head, loosening his thoughts around this meaningless hurdle in the conversation. He pressed on. "Why did you publish this?" he said. "Who came up with the idea?"

Marigold turned from Mansfield to me, then to a poster of the cover on the wall, then back to Mansfield. "When an opportunity like this lands on your desk, you run with it. Any other print publication in the city would have done the exact same thing if they knew what was good for them."

"But why?" Mansfield pressed.

"Why what?" Marigold replied.

"Why print this photo with this headline, calling for the murder of the coin collector?" he said.

"It's fascinating, yes?" they said. "It really makes you think. Who is this man, and why is he entitled to so much wealth? If his death would bring about a greater redistribution of wealth, our society would be all the better for it, no?"

"That's not up for us to decide," Mansfield said. "We don't play such games when murder is involved."

"Hypothetical murder, detective. Correct me if I'm wrong, but I believe there has to be a body before you can start talking about an actual murder." They paused. "Unless... Are you giving us the exclusive scoop of the death of the coin collector and its ongoing investigation?"

Mansfield clenched his fist. I had thought Mansfield knew his way around an interrogation, but here he was, the foolish buffoon, handing Gerard Méliès' body to Marigold—a juicy scoop for the morning paper—of all people.

"We didn't," I interjected.

"Excuse me?" Marigold said.

"We didn't say anything about a body. We're

here about the paper, the cover," I needed to save this thing, bring it home. "Yes, we know it's good for newspaper sales, but what prompted this to come about? Who placed this thing on your table?"

"Her name is Willow Pendercast, a freelancer," Marigold said.

"Thank you," I replied, and made for the door.

6

We arrived at Willow's run-down apartment shortly thereafter and knocked on the door.

"Willow Pendercast, this is the police, open up!" Mansfield called out.

We waited a moment in silence, listening for the tell-tale sounds of footsteps approaching the door or the mad rush to escape our pursuit.

With nothing explicitly condemning to her name, Willow came to the door. She was short, with shoulder-length violet hair and a large green eye.

"Is this about the paper?" she asked, standing in the doorway in a neon green tracksuit.

"Yes. May we come in?" Mansfield asked as he brushed right past her.

"Of course," she said. "Make yourselves at home."

Mansfield had no trouble on that front, taking a seat in her lounge.

I entered her apartment and followed Mansfield, showing a little more respect for Willow's private domain.

"Would you mind brewing us a couple of cups of coffee, Ms Pendercast?" I asked.

"Sure," she said after a moment's hesitation. She closed the front door and peeled off into the kitchen. "How do you take your coffee?"

"Black, no sugar," Mansfield replied.

"However you take it is fine," I said.

How someone has their coffee says a lot about a person. When you're in the business of investigation, you naturally learn to pry any and every piece of information from them that you can.

Mansfield waited on the couch while I paced the room, gleaming for information that would identify her character. I had a feeling she would be an easy subject to interview. She didn't express any concern or uneasiness for our presence here. This also meant that I had a very strong hunch that she had almost no connection to the murder itself.

She came in with the two cups of coffee. Mansfield's black, no sugar, and mine white with ... I took a sip ... two sugars and ... I took another sip ... a shot of vanilla flavouring.

This was not the handiwork of a cold-blooded killer.

"So what did you think of the article, hey?" she asked as she took her seat opposite us and set down two floral coasters on the coffee table between us.

"It was interesting," Mansfield said.

"Where did you come up with the idea, Ms Pendercast?" I took the lead on this one, as I didn't want Mansfield to butcher it like he did with Marigold.

"Oh!" she said, as though she just remembered something. "It was the strangest thing. I've got something to show you. Wait right here."

She disappeared down the hall.

I leaned into Mansfield and said under my breath, "Do you think she knows? I don't think she knows."

"No, I don't think she does either," he replied. "What do you think she's got for us?"

"No clue," I said.

What she had for us that was connected to the article, to the investigation, was anyone's guess. Good thing we didn't have to wait long to find out.

"This may seem a little weird," Willow said as she reemerged from the hall, "but I had a dream about the article one night, and when I woke up I had this."

Willow sat down and placed a gold coin on the coffee table and slid it over to us.

I picked it up and examined it. "Let me get this straight," I said. "You had a memory about creating the article with the face and the headline ... before you actually did those things? And the coin just ... appeared ... when you woke up?"

Needless to say, the expression on my face in that moment was one of confused skepticism.

There was no way this woman could have killed Gerard Méliès, let alone staged the crime scene the way that it was with its cryptic messages and motives. When you work in this field for as long as I have, you get a feeling that some people just don't have what it takes, even if they've got the motives and the opportunity.

"It's strange, isn't it?" Willow said, confusing our scepticism for a communal confusion as to how the coin came to be.

Everyone knew that coins don't come from dreams just like that. If you wake up from a dream that you want to remember, you need to record it while it's still fresh in the morning. You need to pop a blank in to get a memory out. And the memory which comes out isn't gold or bronze or platinum or copper. It's black. Everyone knows a memory from a dream makes a black coin.

So she wakes up with this gold coin and she's got all these weird ideas in her head, but the only thing, the ONLY thing it could realistically be is a case of dream supplanting.

Dream supplanting, if you haven't guessed already (I know you're not that bright...) is when someone inserts a coin in your head while you're sleeping, so essentially you end up dreaming out their memories without realising it.

Usually when this happens the supplanter doesn't want to leave a trace of them having been there, so the fact that the person who supplanted Willow's dream left their coin behind was very peculiar.

It did however feel consistent with the killer's M.O. (modus operandi, their method of operating, for your information), in keeping in line with their trail of clues in the form of coins, stringing us along. To what end, we couldn't exactly say right now.

And I know you're thinking this whole dream supplanting thing sounds like a precise psychological science. Wouldn't that be nice? But really, it's a wildly unpredictable practice depending entirely on the memory being broadcast and how the sleeper would react to such information.

Based on the outcome of this particular instance of dream supplanting, the killer knew exactly what they were doing, to the point that they had figured out Willow's personality and power of suggestibility before diving into her mind with their coin. This was exactly the kind of link in the investigation which would help us to piece things together to narrow down our search.

Still, we were working on the investigation with no suspects yet on the board. We knew

Marigold and Willow's involvement only so far as the printing of the article, with nothing to indicate anything beyond that.

7

I put the "dream" coin in my slot and everything turned the summer sheen of gold.

I was walking down the main strip, Ringwood Boulevard, past all the theaters which each displayed images of the coin collector's face, the image used in the newspaper. There were kids on every street corner, selling the papers like we would see in the old movies, and they're holding up that same image on the paper, calling out the headline, WILL YOU KILL THIS MAN? over and over again, like a prophecy of things to come.

This memory was staged very elaborately, and I could tell immediately that it had to have been designed in one of the studios of the Cinema of the Mind, which gained its wealth and fame as a direct correlation to Gerard Méliès' work developing the coin and constructing memories as both entertainment and currency.

From here the memory brought me into a car, in the driver's seat, and I noticed immediately the lack of mirrors to keep the origin of the memory unknown. I drove off towards the Ringwood hills with no other traffic on the road and the radio playing a broadcast which was talking about the economy of the coin and the sheer imbalance of wealth in this country.

A deep, resonant voice said, "Who will kill the coin collector? I'm asking this as a rhetorical question, a kernel of an idea to call to action the working class who know only too well the fleeting feeling of coins falling through their fingers and into the pockets of those like Gerard Méliès.

"I know, I know, people will try to persecute me for this, for my specific targeting of the coin collector as the iconic figure of wealth and hedonism and inequality in this society. They will read coded messages in my words which are far-removed from the original words themselves or their original intent. Falsehoods will multiply and chaos will breed chaos in the rabid attempt to maintain the status quo. The ultra-rich elites of the world will have those below them eating out of the palms of their hands, a capitalist brainwashing which has been around long before the memory of coin, when our minds were the soft mush of brain matter and our eyes were twofold and our memories couldn't simply be traded away in order to make the rent.

"So I ask again, and I ask you, each and every one of you listening at home, at work, in your cars, at your gyms, who will kill the coin collector? And I ask you to consider the message of my words sincerely, honestly.

"And I ask you also, am I wrong?"

I pulled the car up near the Ringwood sign up in the hills, the view of this luxurious city built upon coins, and I couldn't help but think about the words spoken through the radio, and in this city of all places, there was the stark contrast between those who held all the coins, and those who had nothing, those who couldn't even remember their birthday or what they did that morning.

As the memory dissolved and the bronze light of day returned, I felt myself playing out Willow's scenario. If I were her, coming out of that memory, waking up with that coin in my hand, I would have had no hesitation whatsoever about putting

WILL YOU KILL THIS MAN? on Marigold's desk, printing that article.

I would also have had no doubt in my mind that the "dream" was supplanted by an anonymous stranger, rather than a spontaneous manifestation of coin in hand. You and I both know better than that.

Someone put her up to this.

Someone with resources and fine memory recording skills.

It looked like Mansfield and I would be taking a trip down to Ringwood Boulevard, down to the studios, and taking a dive right into the Cinema of the Mind.

"What's going on," Willow asked in a quiet voice, "am I in trouble?"

I shrugged. "Depends on where our investigation takes us. For now, all we can ask is that you don't leave town."

She nodded, "okay."

"Thanks for the coffee and the coin," I said. "You've been very helpful." I stood up to leave. "Anything else you can think of, anything you might want to add, give us a call." I handed her a card with my number on it.

As soon as we were out the door and down the hall I told Mansfield about the contents of the coin.

"We find the person who created this memory, we find the killer," Mansfield said.

"Something like that," I replied. "You know, she really seemed oblivious to a lot," I added. "I wouldn't be surprised if they did more than just supplanting this memory into her dreams, maybe they did a little extra to modify her memories, nobody can be that clueless."

"You'd be surprised," Mansfield said with a weird chuckle.

"Nobody should be that clueless," I clarified. "Something didn't feel right."

PART TWO:

THE CINEMA OF THE MIND

8

We were in Neon Johnny's Danger Den, in part to unwind after the day's investigations, in part to get a feel for who's been doing what in the studios which might have led to the memory that was hand-fed to the dreaming Willow.

If there was one thing we knew about this place, Neon Johnny knows things. We were hoping he knew something about the rising tension and the class warfare which had led to this murder, if not something about the hollow coin itself.

His name was John Malkovich, and he was not a man. He was a myth, a legend. He was transcendent beyond his physical form.

He was the clone of an actor from your times, albeit an evolved and upgraded form of the man you know and understand as John Malkovich.

Hell, he's an evolved and upgraded form of life as we know it, as we live and breathe and record our coins.

If Gerard Méliès was famous for his wealth in coins, Neon Johnny was famous for his lack of coins.

He didn't need them.

He had tech which bypassed the need for coins, tech which essentially performed the same function as coins, but without the physical object of the coin. The value stripped from the object, from its material wealth, from its fragility and potential to be stolen or lost or discarded or traded away.

There was an aura of information about him, and a sense of permanence despite his physical form being more machine than flesh.

The place had an air of opulence about it without coming across as expensive or elite. Across from the bar there was a small stage with tables pressed right up against it, and performing there were a trio familiar to regular patrons of the Danger Den.

They were Rodrigo y Gabriela y Hendrix. Three guitarists from back in your day, if you might have heard of them, if you were so inclined to develop a sense of culture and class to take a genuine interest in the arts.

I wouldn't put it past you if you didn't.

But even if you did know who these guitarists were you never would have seen them play together.

And let me tell you, Rodrigo y Gabriela could play the shit out of their acoustic guitars, and Jimi Hendrix could play the shit out of his electric. You could just imagine what would happen when you cloned all three and put them on a stage together.

And that's not to mention how they play their guitars on a whole new level now too.

Do you remember how we only had one eye now as we only need one eye to see more than you could back in your days?

Well, the need for finger dexterity never disappeared. We now have seventeen fingers on each hand. One thumb and sixteen fingers spread across two wrists per hand, eight fingers each wrist and a thumb on the end.

Evolution is a beautiful, beautiful thing.

Which means that these already phenomenal musicians by your standards were beyond brilliant now. Their harmony and intricacies were devilishly good. For a few minutes I let myself relax a bit, savouring a nice glass of white wine and really absorbing the aura of the skilled musicians.

Their hands and fingers moved so fast, their melodies so beautiful, playing from muscle memory what coins just couldn't capture.

They were of the same advanced makeup as Neon Johnny, performing with a sense of carefree vigour. They didn't need the coins to make their living, to keep themselves sheltered and fed, they were revolutionaries resurrected from a bygone time.

There was something beautifully primal about it, almost poetic.

And yet if their technologies went mainstream it would threaten to overhaul the social order and bring chaos down upon Ringwood, before spreading like a plague across the country and eventually the world.

I finished my wine and slid Willow's coin across the bar to Neon Johnny.

"It's on the house, Detective Quinn," Neon Johnny said, rapping his knuckles on the polished mahogany countertop.

"This isn't for keeps," I said. "I'd like to know if you have any idea where this might have come from. Actually, two things." I held the coin tight between thumb and forefinger and I leaned in closer and dropped my voice. "Have you ever heard of a hollow coin?"

He furrowed his brow in thought or confusion. "You know what, I don't think I have." He poured a drink for himself, whiskey on the rocks. "And I'd remember something like that for sure."

"I know you would," I said.

He topped my wine up and we clinked glasses.

"What's the context?" he asked.

"The coin collector's dead," I said. "His coins have been wiped blank."

Neon Johnny let out a long sigh. "Of course," he said. "It was only a matter of time before the technology failed. But where does the hollow coin come into it?"

"There was a message at the crime scene. BEWARE THE HOLLOW COIN. YOUR MEMORIES WILL BE REDUCED TO NOTHING. We don't yet know exactly what it means," I said.

"Well I got no fuckin' idea either," he replied. "I mean, we could throw some guesses around as to what it might mean, but I know you cops don't operate the law on guesswork. I sure as hell haven't heard talk of hollow coins before, certainly nothing to the extent of destroying memories. What are you thinking?"

I tapped my glass and thought it over a moment. "It sounds to me like some sort of device which reprograms the coins and renders them useless. The hollow coin would have to be what stripped the coin collector's coins of their memories. It has to be. It's the only thing I can think that would make sense. I'm sure you're thinking it, Mansfield's thinking it. Hell... I think even the reader is thinking it."

"Huh?" Mansfield said.

"Never mind," I muttered. But I knew you were probably thinking along similar lines this whole time. A lot of this work is like a card game. You've got to be selective with who you show your cards to and who you hold them back from. Neon Johnny was one you show your cards to. And your coins.

I passed Willow Pendercast's coin over to him. "Do you reckon you'd be able to help us figure out where this coin came from?"

He examined it closely. Looking for what, I couldn't be sure.

"I'll see what I can do, Quinn," he said as he rolled the coin effortlessly across his row of knuckles. When it reached his thumb he flicked it into the air and caught it in his palm. "I'll just go watch it out back, want to join?"

As he didn't have a coin slot in his head like the rest of us (Slotless, we called them) he had a similar home movie setup to the coin collector, although we assumed his equipment was used far less often.

"You want to give it a watch, sergeant?" I asked Mansfield.

"Yeah, probably should," he replied, and followed Neon Johnny around behind the bar and out into his back room theater.

I stayed at the bar, already having the memory sitting fresh in my mind, giving me a bit of time and space to think the case over. Or just enjoy the vibe of the Danger Den while I waited.

Rodrigo y Gabriela y Hendrix wrapped up their set and cleared the stage for magicians Penn and Teller, performing their sleight of hand and coin magic routine. Now, let me tell you (I've seen it before) if you think their five-fingered magic is good, then these clones with their combined 68 fingers across four hands with eight wrists... It's enough to fool the evolved eye, no matter how many times you review your memory of the performance.

Last week they had Houdini and Copperfield doing a double feature. As much as you learn to trust in your coins as an officer of the law, some of these truly talented folks teach you a thing or two about what you know and what you think you know.

The take-away message is this: question everything.

You don't get to be top of your field and sticking with it for thirty years if you come to believe everything you see as fact.

9

When Mansfield came back from the theater behind the bar, Neon Johnny hung back, standing in the doorway. He sent a friendly wave my way which I returned, and then Mansfield peeled me from my seat and made for the exit.

"So what was his take on the coin?" I asked as we got back into the squad car and pulled out onto the boulevard.

"He said he thought it was a Red Herring production," Mansfield replied. "What with the way they tend to operate, producing memories which aren't quite what they seem."

"So what you're saying is that the memory feels like it seems like it's about killing the coin collector and the resulting social collapse of currency and wealth, but it's really about something else?" I asked.

"Precisely," he replied.

"And what do you think it's meant to be about, if not the death of the coin collector and the social collapse?" I probed.

"Wouldn't have a clue," he muttered. "And that goes for Neon Johnny too."

"It's all very cryptic, very strange," I said.

I made sure to look at my reflection in the side mirror to check I wasn't still in a memory. These things happen from time to time, especially when you're in a position of authority like we are.

We passed beneath a giant golden archway into Red Herring Studios, the studio logo bright and large in the middle of the arch, a red fish passing through an ornate golden wreath, the studio name etched into a banner beneath it. The colours shimmered rich and full in the bronze daylight, and we pulled up to a security gate where we showed our identification to a guard.

"Welcome to Red Herring Studios," they said, taking our badges and inspecting them. "You're welcome to go wherever you want and talk to whoever you want, we won't disrupt your investigation. All we ask in return is that you don't interrupt any recordings which may be taking place." They handed the badges back and lifted the boom gate to allow us through. "Oh, and one more thing," they said as we were about to drive through. "Be careful around the Spidermen, they take their work very seriously."

We drove through, wondering who or what the Spidermen were, but as we passed several buildings on our way to administration, we caught a glimpse of them.

Around the corner of a nearby building, coming out of the door to a set, there was one of the Spidermen walking on candystripe legs. It was impossibly long and thin, contorting itself to fit through the door. It had a vaguely humanoid thin black torso, with arms black like the web of shadows they cast. Four legs and four arms so long that it could scale any of these large boxy buildings with ease. We drove past and it turned its midnight black head in our direction, and I couldn't say if the thing had eyes or a nose or mouth at all.

It seemed like it was always watching, even after we had driven off out of its line of sight.

We pulled up into a parking lot outside of the administration building, and we already had the impression we would probably get lost in here, doubtful whether we would find any of the answers we were seeking, regardless if those answers were here or not.

10

In administration we were sent down a labyrinth of long hallways decorated with posters for Red Herring's most famous works in the Cinema of the Mind. Much of what they produced were detective and crime thrillers, murder mysteries, that sort of thing, where other big budget studios handled more of the straight up action, comedy, or drama releases.

This industry was booming, so long as there were stories to be told, people wanted to buy themselves a piece of the Cinema of the Mind.

And the thing with the coins which played these cinematic memories, they felt so real and authentic while they're in your head, they're far more vibrant and captivating than any of your two-dimensional (or three dimensional, for that matter) films could be.

With all these long hallways and all these posters which looked the same as any other, it felt truly surprising how anyone got to where they needed to go in this building.

All we were going off were the vague directions from the lady at the reception counter, and we had to just keep an eye out for the door with the gold plaque which read PRIMROSE.

There were no doors we could see for a very long time. We figured it must have been the only door in this maze of halls and that it was buried in the back somewhere. We also felt that we would probably have to refer to our memories of these halls to figure out how to find our way back without getting lost all over again.

We found the Primrose door somewhere in the maze, long before the corridor's end.

Mansfield knocked twice before a soft voice called out, "Come in."

In the office there were all sorts of awards and accolades, and at the desk there was a very tall and slender figure processing data on their computer. The screen glowed haunting upon their face and they glanced up at us for a moment before returning their attention back to their screen.

"Just a moment, officers," they said. "Take a seat."

We sat across from them at the desk. I noticed a plaque sitting there with "Primrose, Chief Administration Officer" written on it. Their face was ghostly pale, platinum blonde hair raining smooth down past their shoulders, and their eye was a rare rose gold, leading me to believe it was a modification rather than the work of genetics.

After another moment they turned away from their screen and stared at each of us. First at Mansfield, then at me.

"What brings you to Red Herring Studios, officers?" they asked.

"We're trying to track down the director who made this," I said, holding up Willow's coin. I placed it on the desk and slid it across.

"I'm sorry, Officer..."

"Quinn," I filled in. "Josephine Quinn."

"I'm sorry, Officer Quinn, but I'm the chief administration officer," they said, picking up the coin to inspect it anyway. "I don't concern myself with familiarising my directors' work. I couldn't tell you personally."

"Could you get us a list of directors who have been working for you within the past six months?" I asked.

They turned back to their screen and had a list of names for us in a moment. They turned the screen so we could see. The list contained all their directors along with the films they had made in that time frame.

"Thank you," I said. "And do you have someone here we could go to in order to narrow our search down? Maybe someone who could inspect this coin and suggest who might have made it?"

They nodded then pushed an intercom button. "Barbara, can you have Milton assist the detectives in their investigation on-site?"

"Can do," Barbara replied.

"There we go, officers," Primrose said. "Is there anything else I can do for you?"

"Just keep your line open should we have any more follow up questions," I said. "Thank you so much for your time." I reached a hand across the desk to shake their long and slender hand, which they extended in strictly the most minimal of professional courtesies.

"Of course," they replied. "Anything I can do to help the hand of justice."

We retreated from Primrose's office with the feeling like our presence here was going to be a waste of time. This Milton character could possibly be a setup just to give us the run around. If there was something to hide in this place, they would do everything within their power to keep it hidden, knowing we would do everything within our power to sniff it out.

11

Milton had long dark hair and slender limbs, a somewhat gaunt face which made me think perhaps he was related to Primrose. He met up with us right outside her office almost immediately after we came out, leading us to believe there was some sort of trick of light or mirrors to this hall of hallways.

He was dressed sharply in muted colours and led us effortlessly through the twists and turns, not back to reception, but to a back door exit we hadn't seen before, which seemed to blend simply into the hall. We were sure that we wouldn't have seen such an exit even if we were looking for it.

And while it couldn't have been long that we were in the administration building, it felt good to breathe fresh open air.

"What can I do for you, officers?" Milton asked.

His query felt rehearsed, like he had been through this before.

"We'd like you to inspect this," I said, passing Willow's coin to him. "We need to figure out where it might have come from."

"Very well," he said, rolling up his sleeves and placing the coin into the slot in his head.

We waited beside the administration building, near the parking lot, while he viewed the memory, and Mansfield and I watched a number of Spidermen passing by, going from set to set, a slow and steady amble with their candy-stripe legs, their black bodies swaying from up on high, arms dangling loose and thin, swinging just above the asphalt.

The coin rolled out from Milton's eye and he blinked and gazed back up to us. We waited for him to speak, but he just stood there, holding his gaze.

"Well?" I said. "Anything?"

His mouth peeled into a wide, toothy grin. "Thanks for returning this coin back to me," he said.

"This is your coin?" Mansfield asked, as though the words somehow got muddled on the way from Milton's mouth to Mansfield's ears.

Yes boss, that's what the man said.

He nodded. "This was, perhaps, the single strangest commission I've ever done."

"So," I said, feeling the excitement which came with an impending breakthrough in the case, "who hired you to make this coin?"

His grin remained strangely wide, such that it may have even grown wider. "That's part of what made this job so strange," he said. "I truly have no idea."

12

"What do you mean, you don't know? Where did the job come from? What was your method of communication? Payment? Drop off? Times, dates, places, we need the details," Mansfield demanded.

Again, my boss was getting ahead of himself, as if he were forgetting what sort of crimes we were dealing with. As Milton answered, I felt like I could have spoken for him, I knew already where he was going.

"Like I said, officer, I don't know. I have no idea. I literally have no way of knowing," he replied. "You sec..."

"You gave up all your coins of them once your correspondence was up," Mansfield cut in. "Of course."

You've got to love him. Always a little slow on the uptake, but he gets there in the end.

"That's it," Milton admitted. "The fruit they dangled before my eyes was so ripe and sweet, I couldn't not pluck it."

"More coins than you could dream of?" Mansfield guessed.

Milton shook his head. "Didn't you see? Coins are going the way of the brain. It's only a matter of time. Beware the hollow coin," he said. "Your memories will be reduced to nothing."

"And how do you know about that phrase," I asked.

"They didn't leave me with any coins of who they were," he replied. "But this was one memory they did leave me with."

This kind of circular evidence was maddening. It felt like we would never get to where we needed to go. We needed to push for a different angle, something to potentially blow the investigation wide open.

"Okay," I said. "So you know about the target on the coin collector. You know about the message of the hollow coin. Do you know about his secret collection of contraband coins? Snuff memories, torture porn, all that sort of stuff?"

He maintained his wide wide grin, which was now super fucking creepy. "Maaaaaaaybe," he replied.

"Okay, can you help us identify where some of this content is coming from?" I pressed.

He snapped from his grin and said, "Sure thing, officer. Where should we begin?"

"Hey boss," I turned to Mansfield, "have you got that list of names Primrose showed us? The Red Herring directors?"

Before he could respond, Milton cut in, "Say no more." And he took off down the road, causing us to follow at a brisk pace, walking in the great looming shadows of the buildings containing the film sets.

We wandered past Spidermen who seemed to be in a constant state of coming and going, some of whom paid no attention to us at all, others who glared at us with a dozen menacing bronze eyes piercing from their abyssal black faces and plenty of blank blue coins rolling between their fingers as they went.

He led us into a studio building where they were filming a movie called Vampire of the Sun directed by Jethro McKnight. The building was set up with a vast array of sets and set pieces which were stunning to behold.

"Oh no, not Jethro McKnight..." Mansfield said.

"Are you a fan of his work, boss?" I asked.

He nodded. "I've got all his coins. Please tell me he's not caught up with all these contraband coins?"

Milton gave a casual shrug and said, "You'll be surprised by just how many big names are involved in the underground coin trade."

"How can they get away with it?" Mansfield asked.

"With great power comes great corruption," he replied. "They're invincible. It's Ringwood's worst-kept secret, but no one can touch them."

"But that's what we're here for," Mansfield said,

gesturing between me and himself. "We can do something about it."

I rolled my eyes. No wonder we had never got anywhere trying to shut down the contraband coin rackets. Sergeant Mansfield Trudeau really had no idea how these things worked. Whatever names did come up were either dismissed instantly due to a lack of evidence and pressure from the district attorney's office (bribes) and the sheer pressure from the media blowback of a so-called false accusation.

The last thing we needed was an army of celebrity lawyers rallying against the police department with a string of defamation lawsuits. It just happened that the coin collector's death was the tipping point which forced us to press into this dark underbelly of our much-celebrated city.

I mean, that's one ugly part of humanity which

has stuck around since your times, and well before.

People have always had their secrets.

And people put their own needs above others.

You've seen it before. You know what I'm on about, right?

As we moved through the set of Vampire of the Sun, it became impossible not to notice the lack of actors on set and the lack of Spidermen roaming about behind the scenes.

"Have they wrapped up filming here or something?" Mansfield asked, as he too picked up on the all-too-quiet aura which inhabited this giant space.

"Not quite," Milton said. "Yesterday evening they were preparing for a big day of filming today. This place should be crawling with people."

We wandered past some of the bigger set

pieces and then found ourselves heading down a long, narrow hallway.

There was blood slicked on the walls and we couldn't be sure if it was part of the set or if something else was going on.

At the end of the hall there was a flickering rose gold light coming from a side doorway from an unseen room. In the doorway we saw the room was a massive junk area, littered with props of broken chairs and tables, wrecked cars, trains, and planes. This set gave us no indication as to what type of movie was being filmed here. The Cinema of the Mind was known for being very strange and surreal, but this set for Vampire of the Sun had such a disconnect from one thing to the next that we couldn't even hazard a guess to make sense of what it was supposed to be.

That's all part of the work that gets done here,

but it bore no relationship with the disturbing scene within the room.

Front and center in this great junk room there was a figure hanging from wires like a puppet, hooks punched through his hands and feet, through his chest, and one through where his eye used to be. His neuron system had been ripped from his head and left dangling by its transmitters still wired through his neck to the rest of his body. At first glance we could have passed it off as a very eye-catching prop, but as we approached, we saw that the body was real. It was the director himself.

Below the hanging body there was a cardboard sign with red painted over it:

THE HOLLOW COIN STRIKES AGAIN. IT SHALL CLEANSE THE EARTH OF ROT, PURGE THE SCUM, AND TURN US ALL TOWARDS UTOPIA

13

Mansfield reported the find to the precinct while I sectioned off the room as a crime scene. I think we both dreaded the response from the higher ups. As if there wasn't enough pressure to solve the murder of the coin collector, now a high-profile director had fallen victim to a similar fate and we were still lacking in any genuine evidence that would lead us to the perpetrator.

"Hey Milton," Mansfield said, "we're going to need you to get Primrose to send our office a list of employees working on this set today, along with your list of those involved in the contraband coin trade. And we need to find out what you know about them."

"So basically everything," Milton replied. "I'll

head down there myself once you're done with my help here, and I'll give a full report."

"We might be a while," Mansfield said. "Best to get Primrose onto it in the meantime."

I leaned into Mansfield's personal space. "We don't really need him hanging around for this, do we?" I asked, more of a statement than a question.

"He's our guide through this infernal maze of a film studio," Mansfield said under his breath. "I figured we should probably keep him close so long as we're here."

"Oh," I said with a knowing blink of the eye. "You're afraid of the Spidermen and you want Milton as your buffer." I gave him a playful nudge.

"Shut the fuck up, Quinn," he snapped. "Alright," he turned to Milton, "go on then."

He gave Milton the address of the precinct and the name of an officer to take his statement. For now, we had this hideous crime scene to deal with.

14

"Who would do something so fucked up as this?" Mansfield said.

"That's what we're trying to figure out, boss," I replied.

I circled the body and noticed behind the board with the message there was a chest which had McKnight's blood dripped all over it. I leaned in and lifted the lid.

It let out a long and painful screech echoing through the room like a ghost escaping.

A chest of coins glimmering in the dim light of this haunted crime scene.

Blood continued to drip from McKnight's body, now landing on the coins themselves and I felt faintly sick at the thought of placing a blood-stained coin into my slot. The reek of death curling around inside my head, leaving little streaks and flecks of blood through the mechanism to dry and stick and damage my coin slot system.

No thanks.

"Hey," I called out to Mansfield. "Check this out." I showed him the chest. "What's the bet between these coins being blank and being contraband?"

He thought about it a moment. "I'll say they'd have to be blanks. Why else would they create all this spectacle about the hollow coin and destroying the value of the coins?"

I shrugged like I didn't know better, but I felt like my own hunch was a lot better.

For one thing, these crimes felt like they weren't just about erasing the value of the coin. They were also about exposure. Making known the trade of contraband coins, the memories of sick and immoral things, taking them from the shadows just beneath our noses and bringing them to light.

My gut told me without a doubt these were McKnight's personal stash of contraband. And something said he was less virtuous with his collection than Gerard Méliès was with his.

I tossed a coin to Mansfield.

"Alright then," I said. "Let me know what you find."

He slotted it into his head and I watched and waited.

It did not roll straight back. It was an active coin.

I watched his face as the memory played out and his expression turned from mild indifference to disgust, to a look of unfiltered horror. The colour drained from his face as the horrorstruck shock failed to dissipate. It stuck on his face as the moment stretched out painful and eternal.

I waited for the coin to drop but it took its sweet time.

When it fell Mansfield blinked slowly, gazing blankly downward as he remembered to breathe. A tear rolled down his face and he looked back up to me.

"You were right," he muttered.

"What was it?" I asked, although I wasn't sure I wanted to know.

"No words," he said. "There are no words for what was done." The colour slowly began to return to his face. "All I will say is this," he gestured at the mutilated corpse of McKnight, "was a blessing. A blessing compared to what he deserves." He kicked the chest. "Look at all this. Fucking deplorable."

I knew this was going on. The corruption and the level of depravity, I was not surprised at all. I did not expect it to shake Mansfield like that at all. Especially after all he's seen and all he's been through.

Like, I know our duty is to serve justice—fairness and equality for all—but if a few monstrous individuals died before we got the chance to solve the case? I guess that wouldn't be the worst outcome in the world.

Once news of McKnight's death got out, it would be all over town and the pressure for us to find the culprit would only increase.

The headlines tomorrow at the Ringwood Reminder would read: WHO IS KILLING OUR RICH AND FAMOUS? with crocodile tears heavily implied.

I could sense Marigold gushing at her own brilliance already. The big question to come into the media spotlight from this whole string of crimes was whether or not they would pry open the can of worms on the contraband coins and let the public know what their idols had really been up to.

15

Captain Sweetwater arrived at the crime scene shortly after. They walked straight up to the body of Jethro McKnight and poked him with a long thin finger, making him sway.

"I've sent officers to investigate the whereabouts of the people on the list Milton gave me," Sweetwater said. "Reports are starting to come back with similar scenes as this." They pushed McKnight again, sending him swaying awkwardly about again. "Similar messages as this. I think we're dealing with some kind of murder cult."

It was good to finally hear from someone who made some fucking sense around here. Mansfield was more often than not about as useful as a coin to the slotless. And anyone else I met while on the job couldn't be trusted worth shit.

Captain Sweetwater was my idol, my mentor, my hero. They had been in the job longer than anyone could remember because other's memories of them stretched back so far it felt like they had been there forever. They were the only slotless member of the Ringwood Police Department, and they were the only slotless being to have not one eye but two. They were a perfect biclops and taller than any other person I knew.

They were poking away at McKnight's body but while McKnight was a tall man himself, even with his corpse hanging off the ground, Sweetwater met him face to face. They stared at the body with a melancholy and curiosity you just didn't see with other members of the police.

They made me feel and look like a useless piece of shit, and you know how stellar I am at my job, so that puts it into perspective for you. They saw things that even I missed in my investigations. As much as I knew I would never be like Sweetwater, a part of me yearned to be at least a little bit more like them.

"Okay," they said, turning away from the swaying body and addressing both Mansfield and myself. "Have you swept through the crime scene yet or have you been too focused on this big dumb body dangling here?" Sweetwater asked.

Mansfield gazed bashfully at his feet. I felt my neck prickle hot, not because I knew I had let my mentor down. I hadn't. But just the thought of responding to his question which was put so bluntly. It was a big dumb question that didn't really merit a respectable response.

I gave Sweetwater a nod and said, "We were just waiting on your word, sir."

"Well, this body isn't going to un-fuck-it-self-up now. The killer's in the details," he said, practically shooing us off to check the rest of the set for anything which might give this unraveling murder mystery some cohesion.

The killer's in the details was his way of telling us to search harder to find the evidence we needed to solve the case. We had gone from one body and one killer, to two bodies, to an unquestionable amount of victims with an unknown number of potential perpetrators. No names. All the coins we had were either unearthing more crimes (an ever-growing tree of injustice branching out before us) or they were wiped blank.

In cases like this, and I say that very loosely, often we find a dead end where the memories of the guilty parties have been lost or discarded or sunken into the vast system of coins being circulated throughout our world.

You can't imagine how hard it is to find a memory that someone doesn't want found, especially when people fear their own negative memories badly enough, let alone the prospect of having someone else's bad memories rotting their minds into a sickly depression.

Now we were looking not only for a killer or killers, but also for what device or machine had the power to wipe the slate clean, making the memories of their crimes obsolete, leaving not even the inkling of a thought in their heads or in their possession or in the possession of some random person far away, nothing.

How do you catch a killer when there's no memory of them ever having committed the crime?

16

Sweetwater took the lead in searching the film set for more evidence, more clues, while I shadowed them and Mansfield wandered around somewhat aimlessly.

Sweetwater went off back to the entrance of the set, the logical place to start, and began their sweep outward from there. It didn't take long searching through the little streets and alleys within the building before Sweetwater called us all over.

"How did you not notice this when you wandered past before?" they asked.

It took a moment to understand what Sweetwater was referring to. It was all fine for them to pick up on things we didn't, as a lifetime with two slotless eyes had undoubtedly trained them to notice things we wouldn't otherwise recognise, to see through eyes unclouded, as it were.

What Sweetwater was referring to was one of the Spidermen with limbs wrapped around a building, looking practically like part of the set, a movie monster of sorts. They were so good at blending in with their surroundings we didn't think anything of it. We didn't look twice to take note of the blood slicked down the walls and windows, fountained out and dried from the stump where its head used to be.

We could understand how McKnight's body tied in with the hollow coin investigation, but the body of one of the Spidermen just raised more questions.

They served no purpose other than to produce films. They displayed no emotion, they had no lives outside the studios, they just roamed the grounds whenever they weren't put to work.

And here there was the brutal killing of this sinister-looking but docile creature, its head chopped off and slid down the building, sitting on the sidewalk in a puddle of its own viscera. And it was only now, looking at the severed head that I was able to notice the details on the creature's pure black face. There were a series of slits like gills through which it would have breathed and smelled, and there were at least a dozen rose gold eyes on the thing, each with their own coin slot. Through the neck stump where its head was severed, you could see a series of compact neuron systems with which it would have recorded its films.

There was one more thing in this scene which we had previously glossed over: on the sidewalk beside the severed head there was a message scrawled in blood. This should not be surprising, as there was a message waiting for us at the other two killings.

As I read it, however, I felt a cold wave of dread wash over me. It read:

I AM THE HOLLOW COIN. FEED ME AND SEE. MY MOTHER IS JOSEPHINE QUINN—DETECTIVE, OR MURDERER?

PART THREE:

THE OTHER SIDE OF THE COIN

17

I know you want to know the fallout of that whole scene, but believe me when I tell you we will get there... Eventually.

But this is my story to tell, and I'll be damned if some nobody reader from a bygone era will sway me from my path.

We were back in Neon Johnny's Danger Den in his back room theater because we had a motherfucking revolution coming.

When I say "we" I don't mean myself and Mansfield and Sweetwater. I mean myself and Neon Johnny and Milton and a few other revolutionaries working to break the system as we knew it.

You see, my relationships with Mansfield and Sweetwater were a little more ... complicated than

I may have let on. We all wanted justice, but the thing about justice is that we all hold different perspectives as to what that means. Mansfield held a very naive by-the-book outlook which I believed was very outdated and often problematic, depending on where the power of the status quo lies.

Sweetwater, while still bearing the responsibility of a figure of authority, often tried to view their job and their responsibility from a position of objectivity and privilege, such that their power was not as rigid or heavy-handed as it seemed.

While Sweetwater was not explicitly involved in my planning and actions, I often felt like they knew a lot more than they were letting on.

One thing I knew that they hadn't figured out yet was the coin collector's involvement in our plan.

I could tell you all about it, but I thought it would be better left to the man himself.

In the back room theater of the Danger Den the murmur of the revolutionaries died down. The last member we were waiting on entered the room, Gerard Méliès, living and breathing better than ever before. No hole where he had been fatally wounded, but rather, the most notable thing about him was the lack of a hole.

The coin collector stood here before us all without his coin slot, a copy of his former self, a clone.

I must admit, my role in this plan had sent me deep undercover, and I was still coming to grips with the fact that I was not the detective mastermind I had truly believed myself to be. And yet in the same night I was also expected to comprehend that the man whose murder I was investigating was alive in clone form this whole time and had been instrumental in the murder in the first place.

Now I can forgive you if it takes you some time to catch up. I won't even judge you if you have to go back and take rigorous notes to make sure you don't lose touch with the actual events occurring here.

18

Are you ready to move on now?

Good.

Because it definitely won't be getting easier for you just yet. Just try to think of how hard this must have been for me. You really have no idea.

The moment Gerard walked into the back room of the Danger Den the revolutionaries exploded into wild applause. They knew precisely what he did in order to reach this convergence point today.

I was still catching up, but I was fortunate enough that Gerard had brought along the coin that would clear everything up for me.

"Thank you all," he said as he gestured for quiet in the room. "It is a privilege and an honour to be here today under these circumstances. Many of us have worked very hard to reach this point, and risked so much for this to happen, for which I am eternally grateful. There were those of you who had to perform acts of unspeakable horror, to set the pieces in motion to expose the tyranny within the system which has plagued us for so long. There were those of you who had to perform the meticulous tasks of fabricating memories for those key figures we needed to leverage in our favour, a highly illegal and dangerous task considering the people involved and the power they wielded. Not to mention the memories fabricated for our very own revolutionaries in order to protect them in the roles they had to play in this plan. There was so much information which had to be removed and obscured or deleted, created and put back in place, but now we can bring our plan into the light and bask in its glory, and we have pieced together this special little film to bring everyone up to speed. Make yourselves comfortable, folks. This is the finest film I've been involved in. We call it Project: Hollow Coin."

He placed his one coin carefully into the slot of the projector to share this historic memory with the rest of us.

Neon Johnny turned the lights off and the screen blossomed a warm rose gold light.

The scene was apparently set by a memory plant, an unseen, unheard actor who simply observed from a third perspective to capture everything as objectively as possible.

There was Gerard Méliès sitting comfortably in his home at his dining table which was currently being used to spread a variety of notebooks and sheets of paper, littered with crude scrawling across all of them. This scene would have been familiar to anyone who worked in the Cinema of the Mind, as the planning process for such films were very wild and complicated. These plans, however, were for the as yet unplanned revolution. Gerard was scrawling on his plans when Neon Johnny knocked and entered the dining room.

"Ah, Johnny!" Gerard sprung from his chair to greet his friend. "Is it done? Do you have my clone already?"

Neon Johnny nodded and said, "Come on in so I can introduce you two."

Gerard's clone entered the room and Gerard himself took a moment to check it out, wandering around the clone to figure out just how similar they were.

As you would expect, seeing yourself in this manner would feel quite surreal, especially having the opportunity to see yourself from an outside perspective quite unlike your own. It's kind of like a photograph or video of yourself, but also kind of nothing like it at all.

And of course, the one glaring difference between the two coin collectors was the lack of coin slot in the clone.

"You make yourselves acquainted," Neon Johnny said to the Gerards. "Let me get my equipment."

He left the two Gerards in the dining room, the clone just standing there blankly, void of all presence, glazed over with no memories in his system, lacking the very essence of his humanness.

Gerard led his clone over to the dining table and sat him down before reviewing his notes.

Neon Johnny returned shortly after with a big bag dragging behind him. He hefted it up onto the table with a heavy thud.

"May I present to you for your cataloging purposes," Neon Johnny unzipped the bag, "your very own hollow coin."

He opened the bag up and lifted out the decapitated head of a Spiderman.

19

Let's go back to the scene at Red Herring Studios, where I had just been accused of being a murderer in this investigation. And being the mother of the hollow coin, whatever that was supposed to mean. Could you really consider yourself to be at the forefront of a movement if you had no memory of it? Could it be that simple that you've done the work, lost your coins, and are still able to claim the credit?

As I sat in the back room of the Danger Den the question of my precise involvement in this movement burned away at me. I just wanted the confusion to be over.

Because I truly believed that for the past thirty years I had been a masterful detective and that my role in solving the case of the coin collector's murder was genuine. Because while I understood through my supposed role in my supposed line of work that memory fabrication was a very real thing that happened, there were very few people in the world who could do it successfully enough as to pull it off without a hitch.

This was a two-sided problem.

On one side there are so many people in your life to factor in the course correction of a fabricated memory. It digs a lot deeper than supplanted memories in that the changes you create may need to be changes in the memories of countless other people in your life. Not just one simple memory placed in the right time.

On the other side of the coin the problem I had was that if someone had successfully done it to me, I knew of the few people in the world skilled enough to do it, most of them would be residents of Ringwood. And if I scratched that surface a little more, there's no way that I (in my current mental state) could ascertain whether a fabricated self, in my case a fabricated occupation, was by my own design or not.

As I read and reread that sign on the set for Vampire of the Sun, I thought of just a fraction of some of the possibilities which might have been unfolding there. I read the sign over and over again and none of the signals coming my way were positive according to my "self" as I was there believing my life as a seasoned detective.

Sweetwater and Mansfield turned to me for answers, seeing my name on the sign right there, but I had even more questions than they did, and even fewer answers.

"I don't know where this has come from," I admitted truthfully. "All I can suggest is that we try to break down the meaning behind it. Sergeant, do you have a coin we could test on this, um, hollow coin, I guess we should call it?"

"Why do you want one of my coins?" he protested. "Why don't you use one of your own?"

"Because," I said. "If you look at the message we've got here, I've been implicated in this crime. If you want true objective data, then you don't want me to be involved at that level."

Mansfield sighed then began digging in his coat pockets for a coin.

"Step aside," Sweetwater said, "don't bother, Mansfield, I'll get this." They held a gold coin out and inserted it into one of the many coin slots on the grotesque head.

It rolled in, then there was a mechanical ticking sound processing the coin, then it rolled out the bottom onto the sidewalk.

Other than a bit of blood on it now, the coin looked the same as it did going in. As it would. But we didn't typically test the performance of coins on deceased/defunct coin slots if not out of respect, definitely because we never had the need to.

Sweetwater slid the coin back into their own slot, only for it to slide out again a moment later.

"It's gone," they said. "The memory is gone."

So we came to the realisation there and then that whoever was doing this—killing high profile celebrities and filmmakers and wiping their memories—whether it was me or not, we now had some understanding where the hollow coins came from, what they were, how they worked. One large part of this bizarre mystery was solved. Albeit, served up to us on a silver platter.

"I guess now you'll want to take me into custody before you clear my name from this investigation?" I said.

Sweetwater nodded. "Sorry Quinn," they said. "We've got to follow the protocol on this."

20

I never made it back to the precinct for further questioning.

In fact, I didn't even leave the building with them.

This was right about the time when Neon Johnny arrived on set with his good friend Gerard Méliès. The slotless clone version, of course.

"Stop right there," Neon Johnny said, causing us to take pause and acknowledge their presence. "Josephine Quinn will be leaving with me because, as you can see, the coin collector Gerard Méliès is not dead. You're investigating a non-crime here."

"What about the murder of Jethro McKnight? We're not sure of her involvement in the crime which led to his murder," Mansfield said.

He really needed to think before he spoke.

"Impossible," Neon Johnny replied. "Detective Quinn was with you the entire time, Sergeant Mansfield, was she not?"

Mansfield murmured in agreement.

"Besides," he added, "I've got fresh information on the investigation I'd like to share, but I'll only talk to Quinn."

"I insist that I remain present during these conversations, Neon Johnny," Mansfield said.

"I don't know how you're going to manage that, when you'll be too busy taking my friend Gerard Méliès here to the station to take his statement. Surely you're not going to turn him down, are you?" Neon Johnny said, indicating to me that I should join him before the others could make up their minds.

HOLLOW COIN

"Captain," Mansfield said, "you can't be fine with this. Back me up here, please sir."

Sweetwater gazed from Mansfield to myself to Neon Johnny to the clone of Gerard Méliès. They nodded in agreement with the two slotless men and said, "I'm sorry Mansfield, but I think we need to hear them out. I trust Quinn to handle things in our absence. Do you not?"

Mansfield shrugged it off and gestured for me to follow Neon Johnny out of the building.

I had a million questions for him but I didn't know where to start.

When we went out into the fresh air I went with the obvious. "What do you know about my involvement in this investigation?" I asked.

"You're not a cop," he replied.

"What do you mean?" I said. "Of course I'm a cop. I've been investigating the coin collector's murder. You can't tell me that wasn't real. Or that the past 30 years weren't real."

He shrugged. "I mean what I say. You. Are. Not. A. Cop. Far from it. Deep in your bones, you're a rebel, an anarchist, a bona fide revolutionary hellbent on overthrowing the system which has plagued this society with its obsession with coins and memories, rotting so many minds to ruin."

I stopped in my tracks. My mind was doing all sorts of mental gymnastics, trying to keep up. The Spidermen carried on from set to set moving around and above us, legs curling and sweeping past as I contemplated my own identity.

"I know this must be difficult for you," he said. "You've just got to trust me on this. After all, it was your idea to fabricate this persona and dive deep into the Ringwood Police Department."

I felt fractures forming in my neuron system at the thought of a self who was independent of who I believed I was. An identity which was both me and not me at the same time. This self which felt so real, now turned out to be fabricated.

Was it nothing more than a grand illusion? Where is this real self from which I was born? How can I possibly return to that old life after having it ripped so decisively from my being?

I felt like both versions of myself were now dead, decaying things. My new self was an identity carved from their remains, not in contrast to, but a product of their departure.

"Can you take me home?" I asked Neon Johnny.

"I don't know what you're hoping to find there," he said. "But it won't help your situation at all. I won't stop you, but we've got a gathering at the Danger Den tonight, and it'll clear everything up for you, I promise." He held my hand and squeezed it. "You've been instrumental in building a future we believe in, Josephine. We need you to be a part of it."

"But I don't know who I am anymore," I said. "I don't know what to believe."

"Let me show you," he said. "I put my trust in you before this whole complicated thing started, and you pulled through. Now all I can ask is that you give me the opportunity to show that you can trust me too."

I felt both that I could believe him and that I had little choice in the matter, so I agreed.

21

We're cutting back to the Danger Den, where the coin collector arrived after clearing his name with the Ringwood Police Department. If only they knew the whole truth.

You can be damn sure Gerard only told Sweetwater and Mansfield what they needed to hear and nothing more. Not the coin which would reveal it all, not my involvement, nothing. Even the story of how he happened to be cloned in the first place and killed was left at a minimum.

And of course this was all planned out well ahead of time, as we saw on the screen as Neon Johnny explained how the Spiderman head had been hacked to create a backup of every coin that was fed into it and would wipe the coin clean in the process.

If you didn't take the backup from the head, the memories would rot away with the beast itself.

With a man like Gerard Méliès, the vast quantity of coins could not be sorted before the rot would set in. Part of his process was the lengthy copying/deleting of his collection, swapping out one hollow coin device for the next.

The other part of the plan was to create a movement that would unfurl the total erasure of the coin/memory system. What better way to capture the attention of the masses than by killing the most well-known public figure in Ringwood?

Neon Johnny knocked on the door.

Gerard looked up from his work, forming his plans and cataloging his coins.

"I've got someone I'd like you to meet," Neon

Johnny said, before bringing Josephine Quinn in.

I considered her in the third person because this Quinn being projected from the coin in the Danger Den was the version of myself before I "became" a detective. This was the version who decided to forget everything and become a cop to move this cause forward.

"I'm Josephine Quinn," she said, calm and confident in the presence of this wealthy and powerful man. "From what I understand, you'll need me to pull off your plan."

My head was spinning again (or spinning still) hearing myself behave quite unlike the cop I thought I was. If my being was brought about by fabricated memories, I began to wonder if this coin was authentic too. I had no concrete reason to doubt why this would be another fabricated memory, but when your existence is thrown into doubt, I think it's in your nature to question everything. Far more than you would as a seasoned detective.

"It's nice to meet you," Gerard said. "So you're going to be our undercover cop?"

Quinn nodded. "I'm prepared to do whatever it takes to usher in the new world."

"Whatever it takes?" Gerard said with a soft chuckle. "Neon Johnny has confirmed with me that he has the means and the people to fabricate such an identity to send someone deep into the Ringwood Police Department." He leaned back in his chair, left his plans for the moment, and he let out a heavy sigh. "We need you to understand that this is a very serious and very real and very permanent change that you would undertake."

Quinn stood there silently, staring at Méliès with an unbroken focus.

"You would lose completely your current self," he continued. "And your new identity would consume your life. You would be living and believing a lie."

"I understand," Quinn said. "But I also understand that the way forward is slotless, where memories cannot be bought or sold or traded or lost. Could you make me as I am now into a clone, much like yours which will replace you when all is done?"

I felt so self-conscious sitting in the Danger Den with a group of people who I felt to be mostly strangers, hearing myself discussing the possibility of becoming a clone.

My detective mind played out the scenario of what would happen if my former self went ahead and made a clone. In this future they would hold their revolutionary spirit close to their heart and true to their self, where I was a manufactured dream, the fake, the one who was made to perform a set purpose in this grand scheme.

And now, essentially, my purpose had been fulfilled. I had reached the end of my service.

Gerard didn't respond.

22

I scanned the room to see who else was there. I thought if they did indeed clone me then my clone would surely be nearby, and that they would be truer to my original self than I was.

The thing they don't tell you about fabricating a whole new identity is that you become quite attached to it. The fact that I had originally signed up to give up my identity came as such a shock, I just couldn't fathom how my life would play out from here. I felt like I couldn't just undergo such a drastic change again to become more like my former self, and it would be impossible for me to carry on with my current identity while it came at odds with this revolution I found myself in.

If there was a slotless version of myself in this

room there would be no need to keep me around once everything was done. Did I make that bargain before I became the detective?

I felt like the more pressing question was this: could I afford to hang around and find out?

The follow up question was this: where could I go now?

I couldn't go back to work and move on like nothing had happened, and I couldn't turn on Neon Johnny and Gerard Méliès because I was a large part of their plans too. If I threw them to the cops I would surely be found guilty too, and by showing me this film of theirs, they knew they had guaranteed my silence.

There was also a large part of me which believed that what they were doing, dismantling a corrupt system, was the right thing to do.

They had handed evidence of contraband coins in high profile circles to the Ringwood Police on a silver platter. Those who weren't killed off like Jethro McKnight would be locked up for the rest of their lives.

I also understood why Neon Johnny and Gerard Méliès couldn't stop there. As soon as you cut the head off the snake, three more pop up. The corruption would not end so long as coins could be made and traded.

The tangible coin was a gateway for memories of torture and abuse to be trafficked behind closed doors.

No coins would mean the entire network would have to change, and in that time I knew Neon Johnny and Gerard would be trying to work their influence and impose some protection to those who would be targeted and victimised.

This was all without mentioning that the coin memory currency system was deeply flawed and had created a chasm between the rich and poor that couldn't be crossed, and as I was one of the many folks in Ringwood living paycheck to paycheck I could most certainly see the desire to level the playing field, so to speak, give the working class something to fight for. And if a few Spidermen and rich elites had to die for this to happen, so be it.

If all this had to happen outside the jurisdiction of the law, so be it. I mean, if anything, this showed that even the law, which by its very essence exists as an unbreakable societal bond, could be infiltrated and broken through sheer will and skilled memory fabrication, then what's to stop this happening in the hands of others with selfish and sinister intent?

As I watched the film and struggled to decide whether to wait and see what would happen to me or whether I should take leave and lay low until this all blew over, I came to think about how peculiar it was that this whole thing came about because a rich and powerful man decided to take action, to reduce his wealth to nothing, and the wealth of his colleagues and friends to nothing.

My detective brain was spinning in overdrive, and I knew just how fragile this revolution was and how so many paths within it were leading to violence and/or death. Whether it was my own or so many others, it didn't matter at this point.

The cause was only powerful in unity, and that unity, like everything else in Ringwood, was fabricated. So many coins, so many dreams, so many truths twisted and distorted. This revolution had one thing going for it at this very point in time: momentum.

I stood up to leave, as I was convinced there was a woman across the room who was the spitting image of myself, and that meant I would surely be disposed once I had had one last moment to bask in the success of my abstract performance.

23

I went back out into the front of the Danger Den, heart pounding as I felt as though all eyes were on me, the one person abandoning this great crusade. It seemed like my end would be up, surely these people would not let me go quietly back into the world knowing my warped role in this plan and knowing that I could spread the truth of their goings-on to the public and start an all-out class war in Ringwood.

And we all know how that would play out.

Instead, as I slipped my way around the bar, a hand gently curled sixteen fingers and one thumb upon my shoulder.

"Please," they said, "would you mind staying back for a drink?"

The voice was Neon Johnny's, and before I knew it we were seated at a table farthest from the bar, the stage, and the exit, and we each had bright cocktails poured and garnished with fruit.

"I know this has been a lot for you to process," he said. "But I want you to know that we wouldn't have done this to you unless you were 100% on board and knew what you were getting into. Even though your new identity would not be aware of any of this."

He reached out to hold my hand. The smile on his face held no hint of a threat, and while I had been deceived so much in such a short space of time, I felt that his actions here were genuine and reassuring.

"What's going to happen with me now?" I asked. "What plan did my former self have for me once all this was done?"

"You want to know if she made a clone of herself to replace you?" he asked.

I nodded.

He laughed and said, "No, that would have made things far too complicated." He squeezed my hand. "There was no need for another Josephine Quinn. The only reason Gerard took that path was because he wanted to dispose of his wealth and bring it to the public's attention in the most attractive way possible."

"Okay," I said. "But this all seems so out of character for the coin collector. I mean, if he spent so many years accumulating his fortune, hoarding it from the rest of us, why would he all of a sudden want to wipe it all to nothing and destroy the means for his wealth in the first place? If I were a detective, I'd be suspicious that someone amongst your ranks decided to fabricate a new coin collector like what you did with me."

"I knew you were switched on," he said. "Right from the moment I met you. Well before we fabricated a detective's life for you. Yes, we made the coin collector into a kinder and more generous man."

"How many people know about what you've done? Who you've changed the coin collector into?" I asked.

"Just the few people I needed to make the coins to convince the coin collector to give up his wealth for the greater cause," he replied. "It would spoil the others if they knew such power and influence could be corrupted so easily."

"And you're okay with that?" I asked. "You're fine abusing your own power and responsibility to bend his life to your will?"

He nodded. "For too damn long these folks have corrupted society for their own personal gain. You've seen the coins, the victims of abuse are the young, the weak, the poor, and the different. There is no line they won't cross. Even the coin collector who behaved so noble and pure, collecting the contraband coins to remove them from circulation. You saw the size of that collection. He was never going to do anything about it. He was never going to save those people or get retribution for them. As rich and powerful as he was, he sure was never going to spread that wealth around. He was never going to be the catalyst for change in this world. He was just going to sit there and watch it all burn around him."

I thought about it. I could definitely understand where he was coming from, even if his morality was blurred.

"You understand," he said. "We couldn't have done it any other way. These were the compromises we had to make. You and I made our choices, and Gerard made his choice too. So did Jethro McKnight. He made the wrong choice and now he's paid the price."

"I just want to go home and carry on with my life," I said. "But I know that's not going to be possible."

"I'm sorry," Neon Johnny said. "I wish this hadn't been so hard on you. But there's one more thing I need to show you. It'll be great, I promise. You just have to trust me." He slid our glasses to the side of the table and invited me to stand up and leave.

24

We took a drive in his car out to his home. Up in the Ringwood hills, and it was strange to think how he could afford such a home with such a resplendent view.

He said it was his greatest accomplishment as well as his greatest regret, using what wealth and success he had made from his innovations to perpetuate the cycle of elitism which had poisoned this place. He, like Gerard Méliès, was complicit in the system of greed and inequality, but he, unlike Gerard, was prepared to do something about it.

The Danger Den was for the people.

The revolution was his next step. His big gift to Ringwood. He didn't go into the details of the system which he had been working on for replacing coins, but there was sheer excitement and joy in his voice. He claimed that while he felt so guilty for owning such a prime piece of real estate while so many in this place went homeless, he found comfort in knowing that his home served as a reminder of the fight he was up against, and it was here that most of his great plans had taken root.

It was here that I would find the critical information that taught me who I was before I was a fabrication.

Neon Johnny took me into his home, through its luxurious, yet sterile-seeming rooms. He took me down into the basement where he had been storing this house's heart. All the character and personality pushed into this one space, everything squeezed underground to ensure the rest of the house was purely functional all the time.

There were the family portraits and photo albums, the quaint memorabilia from holidays, handmade coin boxes for those special memories, things you'd usually find in small family homes where there's little else of value.

All the smiling faces beaming out at us, there was Neon Johnny beside Josephine Quinn, one son between them, the most recent picture had the child looking no older than five or six.

"What is all this?" I said, as I felt tears starting to well in my eyes. Although I processed the scene before me, it was all so overwhelming.

"You gave up everything for the cause," Neon Johnny said. "It broke my heart to let you go, but I never forgot a thing. Not even for a moment." He placed his arm gently around my shoulder. He pointed at the child in one of the photos. "This is your son Carlton. Our son. He's missed you like you wouldn't believe. We had to send him to stay with his grandparents until this whole thing played out to keep your fabricated identity intact."

"What was your plan—our plan—when all this was done?" I asked. "How do we piece everything back together?"

He sighed. "Well, there's no going back to the way things were. All we can do is keep pressing forward. We need to make sure real change comes from this. Today we deal with the death and rebirth of the coin collector. Tomorrow we push for the death and rebirth of society. At least now we can work towards rebuilding our lives together, no matter the outcome."

I smiled at the thought. As much as I felt like I was living outside of myself, a stranger looking in, I felt that the intentions were genuine, even though everything felt like it was at odds with my identity. I wanted to embrace this life, but I also knew it would be impossible to pick up where we had left off. We hadn't simply just pressed pause. It felt like a complete reset.

I thought of the idea of having a child that I had no memory of, a living breathing thing I could only assume grew inside me and grew under my protection and loving care.

Was I a loving mother?

Was it possible for me to be a loving mother only to give up all my memories of ever having been a mother in the first place?

The photos were real, genuine. The expressions on our faces could not have been faked.

Maybe I gave up everything because of my identity as a loving mother. Perhaps it was a result of my feelings and emotions that I tried to predict the future for my child and the future in its current state was bleak and harsh and unforgiving.

This was my attempt at course correction.

The longer I thought about it, there was something about the energy in the back room of the Danger Den. I wondered if the people there had come via similar realisations. To be the change which makes the future one worth fighting for.

I leaned into Neon Johnny and gave him a hug.

"You've got no idea how much I've missed this," he said.

"No," I said. "I don't."

25

That night I left my detective life behind. Memories of a life I no longer needed. Coins that were now meaningless, symbolically hollow coins, so to speak. This just left me contemplating the future I wanted to build. With husband and child and revolution in mind.

That night I slept in a bed which was my own, but it felt like the first night sleeping somewhere for the first time. That's essentially what it was.

Neon Johnny slept on the fold-out couch. I felt his love and compassion but the intimacy we once had was gone. If we were to get it back it would take some time. This was the start of something new. Reimagining my relationship with him. He was no longer the informant to my detective ways.

I don't know how he spent all that time knowing the truth about me, about our family, seeing me come through his bar for work and not being able to say or do something.

In the morning I woke to a gentle rapping of knuckles on the bedroom door.

Neon Johnny opened the door a little and poked his head in. "There's someone here I'd like you to meet," he said.

Before he could introduce them, a young child, a boy, came bursting through the door with a large heavy box in his arms and he launched himself onto the bed.

"Mum!" he squealed, dropping the box carelessly on the mattress and collapsing onto me.

He was about six, I think, all elbows and

knees, and he wrapped his arms around my neck, practically suffocating me.

The box spilled open with a tinkling of metal as coins scattered over the bed.

"Mum, hey! I missed you. Do you remember me?" he leaned back to look me in the eye for an honest answer. "Dad said you wouldn't remember me but grandma said that deep down inside there might be a part of you that would."

I gazed back at him, struggling to meet his sheer energy and intensity.

"Carlton..." I said.

His eye grew wide with excitement as I said his name, the expectation that I knew who he was indicating that I had somehow inexplicably remembered my own son.

I shook my head. "Sorry, mate, I lost all my memories. If I could have remembered you, I would have thought of you every day."

His face fell into a slight frown, but his energy was impossibly high. He nodded his understanding. "That's okay," he said. "That's why I brought these!" He grabbed at a fistful of the coins and held them out to me.

"What's this?" I asked.

I figured these were either my own memories I had left behind or Carlton's memories of us which would help me slot back into his life (and Neon Johnny's life too). I didn't want to play up my detective facade for Carlton so I played into his excitement by pretending to have no idea.

Being a mother changes the way you think. I could already feel the tough detective skin melting away for something much kinder and gentler. I felt myself falling into place beside Neon Johnny as a support in his movement.

"Let's watch them right now!" Carlton said. "We've got the projector set up in the lounge room." He scooped up some of the coins back in the box and started climbing out of bed, grabbing and pulling at my arm in the process.

"You remember what I said, don't you?" Neon Johnny said.

Carlton let go of my hand and slipped the coin box on to the floor.

He sighed dramatically. "Not until mummy gets her upgrade..."

"That's right," Neon Johnny said. "You want her to remember these coins forever, don't you?"

Carlton nodded.

"Good, now pop off to the kitchen. I think grandma is making pancakes for breakfast."

"Yay!" Carlton cried out, and raced out of the room.

"What's this upgrade you're talking about?" I asked.

"It's a little hardware upgrade," he said. "It'll turn you slotless and give you unlimited memory. You'll be just like me. This is the goal we've been working towards, ending the cycle of abuse and commodification of memory."

I nodded. "Okay, so who does this? When? And what's going to happen then?"

Neon Johnny revealed a small device about the size of a coin slot with a part that would slide into your head and cover up the slot. "It's all ready to go here and now. We're going to set the people of Ringwood free from their need for coins. Are you ready for this?"

I thought about it for a moment. I felt like I didn't have anything to lose. I felt the trust was there, this was the next logical step in our future. I could move on from my fabricated detective life and reconnect with something more authentic and real.

"I'm ready," I said. "But first, tell me, how long was I undercover for?"

He laughed. "You're not going to believe this," he said. "Four months. It took longer to set up your cover than it did for everything to play out as planned."

26

The pancakes were piping hot and smothered in syrup, waiting for me in the lounge room with Carlton and a woman I assumed was my mother-in-law, and the projector set up ready for the coins.

Neon Johnny brought in the box of coins and I couldn't keep myself from touching the plug which had sealed up my coin slot.

Carlton shuffled across on the couch so I could sit in front of the projector and feed the coins to it.

Neon Johnny placed the box of coins beside my pancakes on the coffee table and said, "Well, what are you waiting for?"

S.T. Cartledge is a bizarro/weird fiction author and poet whose work has appeared and disappeared in various magazines, anthologies, and publishing houses. They share a home with a human adult, human child, two dogs, six cats, and probably hundreds, if not thousands, of spiders and insects. They write and reside in Perth, Western Australia, where they would like to recognise the traditional land owners, the Noongar people of the Whadjuk region, and pay respect to elders, past, present, and future.

ALSO FROM FILTHY LOOT

FILTHYLOOT.COM

CPSIA information can be obtained
at www.ICGtesting.com
Printed in the USA
LVHW111636260721
693716LV00004B/223

9 781087 963488